The Big sister's Tale

Also available from Hodder Children's Books by Margaret Ryan

The Canterbury Tales 1:
The Big Sister's Tale
The Canterbury Tales 2:
The Little Brother's Tale
The Canterbury Tales 3:
The Little Sister's Tale

The Canterbury tales

The Big Sister's Tale

MARGARET RYAN

Illustrated by Adrian Reynolds

Hodder
Children's
Books

A division of Hodder Headline plc

Text copyright © Margaret Ryan 1998
Illustrations copyright © Adrian Reynolds 1998

The right of Margaret Ryan to be identified as
the Author of the Work have been asserted by her
in accordance with the Copyright, Designs and Patents
Act 1998

This edition first published
by Hodder Children's Books in 1998

10 9 8 7 6 5 4 3 2 1

ISBN 0340 714506

Printed and bound in Great Britain by
Mackays of Chatham plc, Chatham, Kent

Hodder Children's Books
A division of Hodder Headline plc
338 Euston Road
London NW1 3BH

For Jenny, with love

Chapter One

One day Mum asked me if
I'd like a little brother.

"No," I said. "I'd rather
have a pony."

But, a few months later,
I got a little brother anyway.
We called him Thomas
Merryweather Canterbury.
Tom for short.

He wasn't too bad at the
start. I remember the first day
I went to see him in hospital.

"Hi, Kate," said Mum.
"Say hullo to Tom."

"Hullo, Tom," I said.
Tom screwed up his face
and burped.

"Mind your manners!"
He didn't.
And, just for being born, he

got lots of toys. He was too little to play with them, so I did. His cuddly blue donkey was my favourite.

I already had it sitting on my bed when he came home from hospital. He didn't notice. He was too busy sleeping...

"Be quiet, Kate, or you'll wake the baby."

Or eating...

"Try not to get the custard
in his ears, Kate."
Or yelling...

"Kate, the baby doesn't want
to watch your video."
10

He was no fun at all.

"Do we have to keep him?"
I asked Mum. "Can't we
send him back?"

Mum shook her head.

"You were just the same at
that age," she said. "He'll get
better as he gets older."

But he didn't. He just slept
less, ate more, and yelled
louder than ever.

I was glad to go to school
to get away from him.

But my peace and quiet
didn't last. Before long he
was in the toddlers' group,
the nursery class, then,
finally, the infant class in
my school.

I had to take him there every morning. He always had a crowd of little girls waiting for him.

"Hullo, Tom," they said, rushing up as though they hadn't seen him for years.

"They're all my girlfriends," he explained to me. What a banana head!

He had only been in school a few months when we had our Christmas concert. Everyone took part, including the infants. They did a nativity play. Tom's two best friends, Usha and Gary, played Mary and Joseph. I was hoping they would come on riding a real donkey, but they didn't.

The donkey was made from cardboard boxes with a furry rug thrown over. You could easily tell. Tom played the inn keeper. He wore a tea towel round his head, tied with Dad's pyjama cord.

Mary and Joseph knocked
at the door of the inn.

"Can we have a room for
the night?" asked Joseph.
"We have
travelled
far, and
my wife
is going to
have a baby."

"Okay,"
said Tom.
"Come in."

It was the shortest nativity play ever. I was totally embarrassed.

"Why didn't you say there was no room at the inn, Tom? Like you were supposed to?" Mum asked later.

"Well, I was going to," said Tom, "but I knew you were watching, and you're always telling me to mind my manners, so I did."

What an idiot!

Not long after that he was
in trouble again.

He cut off Usha's pigtail.

"I was only trying to help,"
he said. "She told me it was
annoying her."

Then he disappeared from his classroom. He went to get a drink of water and didn't come back. Miss Clark, his teacher, sent for me during Art, my favourite lesson.

"Tom's disappeared, Kate," she said, "but he must be in school somewhere. Help me search."

So much for the art lesson.

I had been looking forward to it all week.  We were going to paint sunflowers like Van Gogh.

Miss Clark and I searched everywhere. We finally found Tom tucked behind a coat in the infant cloakroom.

It was the crunching noises that gave him away. That and the smell of hamburger-and-tomato flavoured crisps floating in the air.

18

"What are you doing here?"
I hissed.

"I was hungry for my
crisps," said Tom. "I couldn't
wait till lunchtime."

"What a wally," I muttered,
and handed him over to
Miss Clark.

I hurried back to my class,
but I was too late, the paint
pots were being put away.
The art lesson was over.

The sunflower paintings
were to be part of our display
for parents' evening, and now
everyone had a sunflower
up on the wall except me.

It's not fair!

Chapter Two

It was a very wet Saturday
and we were all indoors,
staring out at the rain.

"I think we should organise our summer holiday to cheer ourselves up," said Mum.

"Good idea," said Dad. "Where shall we go?"

"Let's go pony trekking," I said.

"I think Tom's a bit young for that," said Mum.

"Leave him with Grandad then, or Great Aunt Izzy."

"I don't think Aunt Izzy's cat has recovered from the last time yet," said Dad.

"I was only seeing how the hoover worked," said Tom. "I didn't know the cat's tail was so close…"

"But I DO know where we should go on holiday. Wait there."

Two minutes later he was back, wearing his bermudas and my face mask and snorkel.

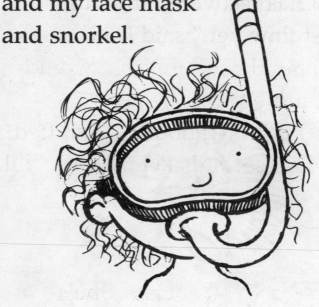

"We should go to the beach," he said.

"BORING," I said. "I want to go pony trekking."

But, of course, Mum and Dad thought a beach holiday would be best. They always do what Tom wants. It's not fair.

Then Mum and Dad had a good idea.

"Why not ask a friend along on holiday, Kate? That would be more fun for you."

"I'll think about it," I sniffed.

Two seconds later, I said, "I'll ask Melanie."

 Melanie's a new girl in my class. She's very shy and has no brothers or sisters. Lucky thing.

Melanie was delighted with the idea. My mum went round to see her mum and it was all arranged.

"I can't wait for the holidays now," I said. "This is going to be great fun!"

How wrong could I be?

Chapter Three

We decided
to go to
Spain for
our holiday.
Mum
bought me
two new
swimsuits
as a reward
for getting
my fifty
metre
swimming

certificate. Tom just had his
old bermudas. He wasn't
keen on swimming.

"I don't like getting water up my nose," he said.

But he wanted Mum to buy him flippers for paddling in. What a wally!

At last holiday time arrived. We all piled into a taxi to go to the airport and Melanie's mum and dad, and our Grandad and Great Aunt Izzy, all waved us off.

There were hundreds of
people at the airport. Lots of
them were dressed like us, in
T-shirts and shorts. Tom wore
his sunglasses as well and
kept bumping into people.

Mum bought Melanie and me a pony book each to read on the flight, and Tom got a colouring-in book and some  felt-tip pens. After that, we boarded the plane.

We fastened our seat belts
for take-off, and Tom sucked
a sweet to stop his ears from
popping. It stopped him
talking too. But not for long.
Two minutes into the air…

"Kate, can you take me to
the toilet?"

We squeezed past the
stewardesses starting to serve
coffee. Everyone looked at us.
Then...

"No smoking in the toilets,
Kate."
Everyone looked at us again.

But that wasn't the worst.

When Tom came out of the toilet, he wanted to know where his wee wee went when he flushed it away.

"Does it fall out of the sky, and rain on people?" he asked.

"I don't know," I hissed, my face scarlet.

"I'll ask the captain,"
he said.

And he did.

Dad took him to visit the
cockpit during the flight and
he asked the captain.

I made Melanie promise she
wouldn't tell anyone at school.

"But I think Tom is really funny," she said.

"*You're* not his big sister."

After a while we arrived in Spain. The hotel we had chosen was very nice, even though Melanie and I had to share a room with Tom. I told him his bed was the one nearest the window. At least, that's how it started out.

Melanie and I got changed for dinner. I felt very grown up eating my Spanish omelette and fried potatoes. Tom had a hamburger, covered in the tomato ketchup Mum had brought from home. For pudding we all had ice cream and chocolate sauce. But, before anyone could stop him, Tom put tomato ketchup on that as well.

Melanie thought this was hilarious.

Not long after dinner we went to bed. Tom went to sleep immediately, ZONK, like he always does. Melanie and I sat up for ages, whispering and giggling and making plans for the next day. Finally, we fell asleep too.

Next thing I knew, I was being woken up by a dig in the ribs from a very sharp elbow.

"What? Whatsamarrer? Is it morning?"

"No, it's me," said Tom. "I don't like my bed any more. I want yours."

I was too
tired to
argue.

I climbed out of my bed and
fell into Tom's. That's how, in
the morning, Mum found me
fast asleep in a bed with sheets
covered in felt-tip drawings.
   "Who did that?" gasped
Mum.

"It's Kate's
bed," said
Tom.

If Mum hadn't been there,
I'd have thumped him.
"Some of those drawings are
really good," giggled Melanie.
"Whose side are you on?"
I muttered.

Chapter Four

It was very hot and sunny that
day, so Tom decided
his legs didn't work.
They worked
going down the
fancy iron
stairway to
have breakfast
on the hotel patio, and they
worked charging round the

breakfast
tables
after his
stripy
ball –

but when we had to carry all
our stuff down to the beach,
they didn't work. Dad had
to carry him and I had to
carry Tom's
bag as well
as my own.

But we had a great time.
I swam about for ages trying
out some new strokes.
Melanie had just learned to
swim and wasn't very
confident in the sea, so she
had a rubber ring with her to
play with.

Tom had on his armbands as
he made sandcastles by the
water's edge. Some elderly
Spanish ladies stopped to
chat to him and admire his
blond curls.

Then they asked Mum if they
could buy him an ice cream.

Honestly, that boy. How
does he do it?

When it got too hot, we
went back to the hotel for
some lunch and an afternoon
nap. Melanie and I fell asleep
right away. When we woke up,
Tom was still asleep in his
own bed, but he wasn't alone.

Tucked up beside him was a
huge red geranium in a big
brown pot.

"TOM," I yelled.
That woke him up all right.
"Why have you got a
geranium in bed with you?"
"I woke up and I was
lonely," said Tom.

"I didn't want to disturb you, so I went down to the garden and brought up a flower to keep me company."

"But this morning you couldn't walk, and now you can carry a heavy geranium pot up two flights of stairs!"

"I like geraniums," said Tom. "Grandad's got them in his window box."

"Isn't Tom sweet?" said Melanie.

"No," I said. "He's nuts!"

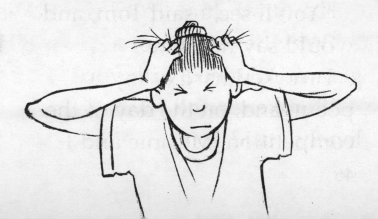

Chapter Five

A few days later, the hotel announced a children's talent competition. I decided to write a poem for it that Melanie and I could recite.

"I'm entering the competition too," said Tom.

"What are you going to do?" I asked. "Sing - dance - recite a poem? You can't do any of those."

"You'll see," said Tom, and would say no more.

I worked hard at my poem, and, on the day of the competition, Melanie and I

46

stood
up to
recite it.
We were
really
nervous,
standing
there by
the hotel
pool
with
all the
grown-
ups

watching, but we did our
poem and it was really good.
It was all about sea and sand
and summer and everybody
clapped when we'd finished.

Some of the other children in the hotel sang songs and danced.

Then it was Tom's turn.

"I'm going to tell some jokes," he said.

"Oh no," I groaned. I'd forgotten about his awful jokes.

And he started...

"What do you get from a nervous cow?"

"We don't know," shouted the audience.

"A milkshake," said Tom.

"Why do elephants have trunks?"

"We don't know," shouted the audience.

"Because they'd look silly carrying suitcases," said Tom.

"Why is a chicken like a plum?"

"We don't know," shouted the audience.

"They're both purple except for the chicken," said Tom.

The audience fell about
laughing and Tom won
the competition.

He got a
certificate
and a huge
Spanish
donkey.

It wasn't fair. I'd spent ages on that poem, and I'd have loved that donkey.

Melanie thought Tom's jokes were great, but *she* doesn't have to listen to them all the time.

We went swimming in the hotel pool after that.

"Keep an eye on Tom, Kate," said Mum and Dad.

As usual, Tom wanted to do something silly. He wanted to put his armbands on the donkey's ears and take him into the pool too.

"Don't be so stupid," I said, then I ignored him.

I swam
away,
diving
down
deep
into the
pool,
enjoying
the
under-
water
quiet.  Finally I surfaced
and shook out my wet hair.
Melanie swam towards me
as I swam lazily backwards.
Then, over her shoulder, I
saw Tom. He was in the pool,
but he didn't have his
armbands on.

They were still on the donkey's ears.

Instead, he was wearing Melanie's rubber ring. But it was far too big for him, and as I watched, horrified, he slipped through it and disappeared under the water.

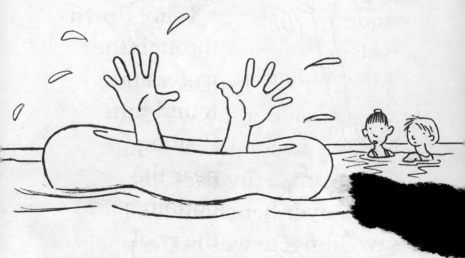

"Tom," I yelled and turned and dived down after him.

All I could think of was that I was supposed to be looking after him. If he drowned it would be all my fault.

I shot down through the water and found him floating near the bottom of the pool.

I grabbed him by
the armpits and
hauled him up
to the surface.

He came up coughing
and spluttering.

When he could speak,
he said, "I hate water up
my nose."

"Silly ass," I said, and held
on to him tight as I dragged
him out of the pool. Then I
hugged him to bits.

"Stop squashing me, Kate,"
he gasped.

Mum and Dad rushed over
and hugged us both. After that,
they gave Thomas Merryweather
Canterbury the row of his life.

Melanie joined in. "You're
a real idiot, Tom," she said,
"wearing a ring that's too
big for you. You could have
drowned. It's only thanks to
Kate that you didn't."

"Quite right," said a lady in
the crowd that had gathered.
"You should be thankful that
you've got such a brave big
sister, young man. Your mum
and dad should be proud of
her."

"Oh, we are. We are," said
Mum and Dad, and hugged
me again.

Everyone made a fuss of me.
It was very embarrassing, but
nice. Melanie said she would
tell everyone when we got
back to school.

"You really are my very best
friend," she said, and linked
her arm through mine.

Then a photographer
appeared and took my
picture. It was in the local
paper the next day.

'BIG SISTER SAVES LITTLE BROTHER FROM DROWNING'

it said, but in Spanish. One of the waiters showed it to me.

Tom was a bit quiet after the row and for once was on his best behaviour.

It didn't last long.

We were on the plane going home, just loosening our seat belts after take-off, when...

"Kate, can you take me to the toilet?"

We squeezed past the stewardesses starting to serve coffee. Everyone looked at us. Then...

"Kate, when you go to the
toilet in the plane, does your
poo get collected in the same
tank as your wee wees?"

Who'd be a big sister????

If you enjoyed reading this Canterbury Tales story, look out for book 2...

THE CANTERBURY TALES
The Little Brother's Tale

Margaret Ryan

One day Mum asked me if I'd like a little sister.

"No," I said. "I've got a big sister and that's bad enough."

Then I though about it. A little sister would be smaller than me. I could boss her about...

Tom is used to being the centre of attention - but now it's baby Annie's turn.

Soon Tom's making plans to win back the limelight - and a family wedding seems like *just* the right occasion!

If you enjoyed reading this Canterbury
Tales story, look out for book 3...

THE CANTERBURY TALES
The Little Sister's Tale

Margaret Ryan

*No one asked me if I'd like a big brother
or a big sister.*

*Kate and Tom were already part of the
Canterbury family when I was born,
so I was stuck with them...*

Annie doesn't think it's fair being the
youngest.

She gets Kate's old clothes and Tom's
old toys.

She even has to share her bedroom.

But Annie's got an idea - and this
time she's going to get her own way!